Inhalant Abuse

Matthew Robinson

rosen publishing's

rosen central®

New York

Published in 2008 by The Rosen Publishing Group, Inc.
29 East 21st Street, New York, NY 10010

First Edition

Library of Congress Cataloging-in-Publication Data

Robinson, Matthew, 1978–
Inhalant abuse / Matthew Robinson. — 1st ed.
    p. cm. — (Incredibly disgusting drugs)
Includes bibliographical references and index.
ISBN-13: 978-1-4042-1958-8 (library binding)
ISBN-10: 1-4042-1958-7 (library binding)
1. Solvent abuse—Juvenile literature. 2. Solvents—Health aspects—Juvenile literature.
3. Aerosol sniffing—Juvenile literature. I. Title.
RC568.S64R63 2008
362.29'9—dc22

                                                              2007004733

Manufactured in China

Contents

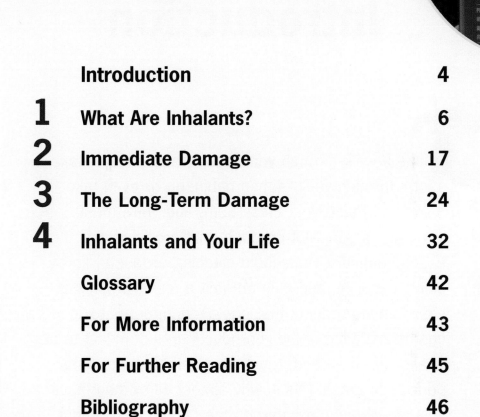

Introduction

ake a walk through your local grocery store, take a look through your kitchen cabinets, or even take a glance around your classroom, and you'll most likely find a bunch of products that are filled with toxic chemicals. Household cleaning products, spray paint, gasoline, and glue are just a few examples of easy-to-find products that contain dangerous toxic chemicals. Most of these products are not meant to be swallowed, breathed, touched, or smelled (for long periods of time). This is why almost all of them have specific warnings printed on their labels that read a lot like this:

Caution: Keep out of reach of children. Avoid contact with eyes, skin, mucous membranes, or clothing. Avoid breathing product. Contact can cause burns. If swallowed, contact physician immediately!

You might think it sounds crazy, but there are people out there, young people no less, who actually choose to do exactly what these warning labels tell them not to do: they purposefully breathe in these products, thereby inhaling toxic chemicals into their mouths, noses, and lungs. Sometimes they even accidentally swallow these chemicals in the process. Gross!

You're probably wondering why in the world someone would do this? Well, the answer is just as sad as it is simple: inhaling toxic chemicals can sometimes give the user a cheap, fast high, similar to that of drinking alcohol.

"But the warnings are printed right on the label! Can't these people read?" you're probably thinking. And, yes, most of them probably can read, but they just don't know all the facts. Or maybe they don't think the warning labels, often printed in big letters right on the front of these products, are telling the truth.

They probably think that just because they can find these products in their homes or classrooms that they're not as dangerous as more well-known illegal drugs such as heroin or cocaine. Or maybe they think that just because the high a user experiences from inhalants doesn't last very long that the damage done to their bodies or their lives won't last very long either. But they're wrong. And if they don't pay attention to the warning labels found on these products soon, they might be dead wrong.

But you're not going to be like them. By reading this book, you're going to find out all the disgusting yet true facts about the dangerous drugs known as inhalants. Put simply, you're going to learn that the warning labels are telling the truth.

1

What Are
Inhalants?

ost of us are aware of the dangers of cigarettes, alcohol, and drugs like crack cocaine, but far too few of us are aware of the similar dangers associated with inhalants. This is surprising considering that, according to the National Inhalant Prevention Coalition (NIPC), one in five American students will use inhalants to get high before they reach junior high school. This means that, whether you're aware of it or not, you probably know a few kids who have risked their lives messing around with inhalants.

But what exactly are inhalants? And how are all of these kids getting their hands on inhalants? And what exactly are these kids doing with inhalants? Let's answer these questions now.

A Quick History of Inhalants
The majority of inhalants used by mankind for the past few hundred years have been used for medicinal

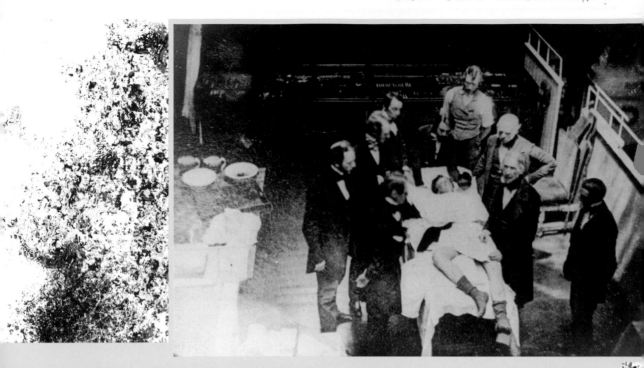

Ether, one of the oldest known inhalants, was first used for medicinal purposes on March 30, 1846, by an American doctor named Crawford Williamson Long.

purposes. In fact, the first widely used inhalant was "laughing gas," invented in the late 1700s and used primarily by dentists. In the late 1800s, doctors began using the gas known as ether to help their patients with pain during surgeries. The amount of people using these inhalants for nonmedicinal purposes was small.

It wasn't until the early 1900s and the widespread availability of gasoline that inhalants became a problem in America. Because gasoline (yes, the same stuff you put in your car) was inexpensive and easy to find, it was mainly the poor and the young who breathed in its toxic fumes to get a cheap, fast high. The 1950s brought with it young people risking their lives by breathing in common household glues in order to get high.

In today's age, with so many products sold on store shelves that can be used as inhalants, inhalant abuse is a serious problem both in America and worldwide.

Making Sense of a Senseless Drug

There are literally thousands of products sold in stores nationwide that fall under the category of "inhalants." An inhalant simply refers to any substance that, when inhaled through the nose and/or mouth, causes a psychoactive effect in the user. While "causes a psychoactive effect" is basically just a fancy way of saying "it makes you high," what it technically means is that the chemicals from the product being inhaled are altering the way your brain is supposed to work, thereby changing your mood and behavior for periods of time—maybe even permanently! And that's not even getting into all of the harm inhalants can cause to other vital organs in your body.

Since there are thousands of products and substances that can be considered inhalants, let's break those products up into four categories to make them easier to understand.

The Four Types of Inhalants

The four types of inhalants are solvents, anesthetics, aerosols, and nitrites. Let's take a moment to learn about each one individually.

Toxic inhalants come in many different shapes, sizes, and colors. Always read a product's warning label before using it for a prolonged period of time or in a room without windows.

Solvents

A solvent is anything that can be used to dissolve something else. The most common solvent around is water, since it can be used to dissolve many different substances (such as dirt or salt). Obviously, water is not a dangerous solvent. Solvents become dangerous when they employ complicated and toxic chemicals in order to dissolve whatever it is they're trying to dissolve.

Exploding Lungs

Misuse of a nitrous oxide tank can cause your lungs to over-expand. When you breath in cold, pressurized air, it expands once it warms up in your lungs. Breathe too much of it at one time and your lungs could possibly explode. No joking! Ouch!

For example, to get paint off of a home patio in order to paint it with a brand-new color, you'd need to use something called paint remover. Paint remover carries in it many dangerous chemicals that, when inhaled, can cause you to feel high or dizzy while at the same time damaging many of your vital organs.

Some of the chemicals often found in dangerous solvents are toluene (often found in glue), benzene, methanol, and Freon. Any products containing one or more of these chemicals should be considered a dangerous inhalant and should be handled with extreme care and with strict attention to the instructions found on the label.

Examples of dangerous solvent inhalants include paint thinner, nail polish remover, glue, and gasoline.

Anesthetics

Anesthetic inhalants are usually used in surgeries to either alleviate the patient's pain or make the patient unconscious so he or she doesn't have to experience the surgery. If you've ever had your wisdom teeth or your tonsils removed, a doctor or a nurse most likely gave you some type of anesthetic to help you with the pain. These people went through years of medical training in order to learn how to safely administer anesthetics to their patients. I'm sure you can see the potential disasters in giving yourself anesthetics in order to get high. It's just plain crazy.

Laughing gas, also known as nitrous oxide, an anesthetic primarily used by dentists, can be found in some aerosol spray cans, such as whipped cream canisters and cooking oil sprays. Nitrous oxide has the potential to decrease the oxygen levels in your blood, which can lead to unconsciousness and even death.

Aerosols

An aerosol inhalant is a dangerous chemical liquid held under pressure inside of a canister. The liquid is pushed out of the aerosol canister by something called a propellant (often a chemical such as a fluorocarbon), which on its own can be just as dangerous as whatever liquid it's helping push out of the canister. Many hairsprays and spray paints come in aerosol cans.

While many solvents and anesthetics can be found in aerosol containers, inhalant abusers often prefer aerosols because they think they

Don't be fooled into thinking that spraying an inhalant into a bag and then inhaling it (huffing) makes it safer. Huffing is just as dangerous as any other form of inhalant abuse.

can either spray them directly into their mouths or breath in the "mist" form of whatever toxic chemical they're trying to inhale. These people often find out the hard way just how wrong they are. Aerosols are just as dangerous, if not more dangerous, than all other types of inhalants.

Nitrites

Amyl nitrite is a chemical compound most often used by those with heart problems to help prevent heart attacks. Amyl nitrite quickly reduces blood pressure and causes the user to feel a quick rush. It's usually found in little glass vials that you break open under your nose and inhale. In the 1960s, you could walk into a pharmacy and purchase amyl nitrite over the counter. Vials of amyl nitrite, also known as "poppers," quickly became illegal when people started buying them not just for their health but in order to get high.

Today, poppers and other nitrites are pretty uncommon, but at one time they were a big part of inhalant abuse.

How Inhalants Are Abused

Now that we've learned the four different types of inhalants, it's important that we understand exactly how these inhalants are used. This is not only so we can spot inhalant abuse happening around us (and hopefully prevent it), but also so we completely understand how and why inhalants cause so much disgusting damage to the user's body.

"Huffing" is the primary way most inhalant abusers get these toxic chemicals into their bodies. By pouring solvents, such as glue or paint, into the bottom of a paper bag and then breathing directly out of the bag, the abusers quickly do permanent damage to their mouths, noses, and lungs, coating and eventually diseasing their bodies' most vital organs. Do you think it sounds like a good idea to coat your lungs in a layer of paint? That's basically what inhalant abusers are doing when they huff paint.

Another form of huffing involves soaking a rag in a solvent like gasoline or glue and then placing that wet, chemical-dipped rag directly over

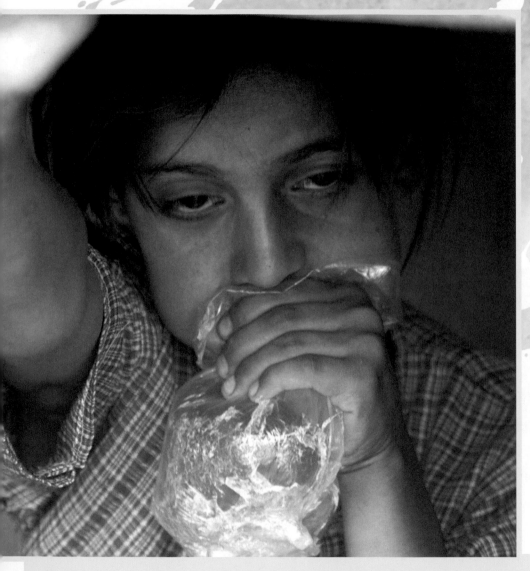

Many homeless children, especially in third world countries, are drawn to inhalants because they're cheap and are sometimes even found in trash cans.

your mouth and nose and breathing in and out for a long time. Gross! It sounds shocking, but people actually do this!

After reading this, you probably won't make the mistake of huffing. By huffing with a rag in your mouth, you can actually end up ingesting harmful chemicals that can poison you, doing serious damage to your body even the first time you huff. Talk about a bad idea!

Another method of using inhalants to get high involves putting an aerosol canister in your mouth and spraying the toxic chemicals right into your body. When it comes to inhaling nitrous oxide, abusers will often put their mouths directly on the pressurized nitrous oxide tanks and breathe the gas right into their lungs. What most inhalant users don't realize is that the air held within a nitrous oxide tank is freezing cold and can actually freeze the inside of your mouth, nose, and lungs, killing the healthy tissue immediately.

"Whippets" are another form of nitrous oxide inhalants, where the toxic gas comes from inside a small little tank as opposed to a large one. Some people either breathe the gas directly out of the whippets or fill up balloons with them and then breath in and out from the balloons. Don't be fooled into thinking that you're any safer breathing nitrous oxide from a whippet or a balloon. There is absolutely no safe way to try nitrous oxide or any other deadly inhalants.

These are just a few of the crazy methods people utilize in order to get high from inhalants. By now you're surely starting to see just how gross and dangerous inhalants really are.

We've learned about the four types of inhalants and their many uses. Let's take a closer look and travel inside the human body to see first-hand all of the extensive damage inhalants can wreak upon our most vital organs.

2
Immediate
Damage

Getting high on inhalants may seem innocent enough at first. After all, most inhalants can be purchased legally, and the high from inhalants only lasts for a few minutes. But don't be fooled: the damage done by inhalants—even after just your first time trying them—can be just as dangerous, long lasting, and deadly as that done by drugs like heroin, crack cocaine, and alcohol.

Since there are so many different types of inhalants and so many different products that fall under the category of inhalants, the many dangers of and damages done by these toxic substances can differ from inhalant to inhalant. The one thing that can be said for all inhalants is that they are all equally dangerous and potentially deadly. Trying an inhalant even just once is like playing Russian roulette with a loaded gun. Let's take a look at the damage inhalants cause to the human body in the short term.

There are few drugs that get into your bloodstream faster than inhalants. You see, when you breathe in oxygen, it enters your respiratory system. The job of your respiratory system is to deliver oxygen to all of the different parts of your body that need it in order to survive, such as your brain, heart, and lungs. Since your respiratory system doesn't know the difference between healthy oxygen and toxic inhalants, it sends the dangerous chemicals found in inhalants to all of your vital organs just the same as it would if you were breathing in normal air. Within seconds of breathing in, the deadly inhalants have penetrated your brain, heart, lungs, kidneys, bloodstream, spinal cord, and many other fragile and important parts of your body.

Because inhalants take effect so fast, the inhalant user will almost immediately feel dizzy, light-headed, disoriented, and tingly. There will often be visual hallucinations. The user's heartbeat will begin to race, and often there is a feeling of warmness or even an immediate breakout of sweat on the user's forehead and hands. The inhalant abuser's ears will begin to ring, a similar feeling one would have after leaving a loud rock club or listening to loud music on headphones. This is called tinnitus, and it can often lead to deafness and permanent damage to the eardrums. While feeling the effects of inhalants, the user will experience a loss of muscular coordination, meaning that it becomes hard to walk, hard to stand up, hard to hold on to things, and even hard to speak without slur-ring words.

In some cases, the effects of inhalants can be so strong that the user temporarily loses control over the ability to blink, swallow, vomit, or

The high from inhalants can cause you to quickly lose control over necessary bodily function, greatly impairing your ability to think clearly or make good decisions.

control his or her bowels and bladder. Basically, it can totally paralyze your body's ability to take care of itself. There are so many scenarios in which losing control of these functions can lead to death that it's impossible to even list them all.

The high from inhalants usually lasts only a few moments (although in some cases it can last as long as a few hours) and is quickly followed by a depression of all bodily senses. The user becomes very tired and

Watch Your
Blood Pressure

Most inhalants cause a severe drop in blood pressure, which is why the user often experiences dizziness and nausea. The technical term for this is hypotension. Hypotension can lead to fainting, chest pain, headaches, and even seizures.

groggy, a similar feeling to how you feel when you first wake up in the morning. This feeling often leads to vomiting, shortness of breath, and irregular heart rhythms. As we'll soon see, symptoms such as these can quickly, and easily, lead to death.

Overdosing

Since it's impossible to know exactly how a particular inhalant will affect someone, or how to gauge how much of the toxic chemical a person is breathing into his or her body with each breath, there is no way to know how to prevent an inhalant overdose. Whether you're just taking a quick huff out of a balloon or huffing out of a bag for a few minutes, an unexpected inhalant overdose can strike at any time.

Sudden Sniffing Death Syndrome

Sudden sniffing death syndrome is a big fancy name for the most common and easiest way to die from inhalant abuse. Put simply, sudden sniffing death syndrome is a massive heart attack caused by inhalant use.

Adrenaline is a chemical released in your brain that puts your body on a high state of alert. It lets you know that potential danger is near and that you better do something about it quickly. Lots of people have learned to enjoy adrenaline. For example, that big surge of excitement and fear you feel when riding on a roller coaster is adrenaline. That shocked feeling you get when your friend jumps out and yells "Boo!" is adrenaline. Your body knows how to handle adrenaline like this. Your heart races, you may even break out into a sweat, but in no way does this type of adrenaline kill you. But when you're high on inhalants, all of that changes.

Many inhalants, particularly anesthetics such as nitrous oxide, can so depress the functions of your body and put you in such an unnatural state of relaxation that your body loses its ability to handle adrenaline. When your body is in such a state, anything loud, shocking, or frightening can send a strong enough jolt of adrenaline into your heart to cause cardiac arrest (a heart attack) and kill you. This is sudden sniffing death syndrome, and it's a very real risk of messing around with inhalants.

If you ever come across someone who is high on an inhalant, do your best not to scare the person, make loud noises, or excite him or her in any way—it could literally kill the person. This sounds crazy, but it should serve as a stark reminder that inhalants are not meant to breathed, huffed, or abused in any way. Those warning labels are telling the truth!

Freezing Your Mouth

Breathing directly from an aerosol canister or anesthesia tank can instantly freeze parts of your mouth, tongue, and internal organs. Since hot air expands, pressurized air has to be kept nearly freezing cold in order to prevent aerosol canisters and anesthesia tanks from exploding. Many people make the mistake of directly breathing in this freezing cold gas, thereby causing serious freezing burns on the insides of their mouths, tracheas (windpipes), nasal passages, and lungs.

If the gas is cold enough, it will permanently and instantly kill any live cells it comes in contact with. If enough cells are killed, you'll have to have surgery to have sections of those body parts removed. Many inhalant abusers have ended up losing large portions of their tongues, the roofs of their mouths, and even entire lungs by breathing in freezing cold gas. Can you imagine how painful that must be? You probably don't even want to think about it!

Trouble Breathing?

Losing the ability to control your breathing is another side effect of inhaling anesthetics such as nitrous oxide. Your body needs oxygen in order to stay awake and keep all of your organs functioning. A large dose of anesthetics can depress the portion of your brain that controls breathing to such an extent that you fall asleep and never wake up again.

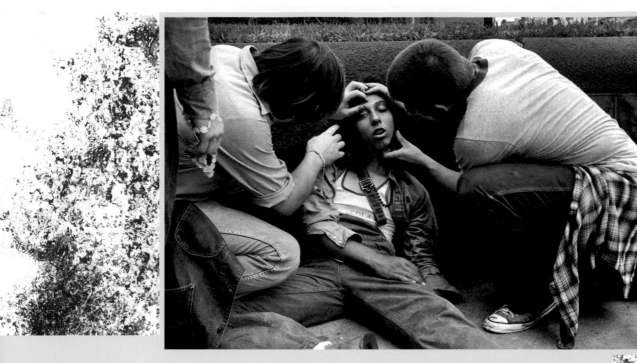

An inhalant-related overdose can come on in a matter of seconds and can quickly lead to unconsciousness, vomiting, and even death.

Some people even breathe nitrous oxide through oxygen masks, just like the ones people in hospitals wear when they need extra oxygen. This is a serious health risk because nitrous oxide is obviously not oxygen. Therefore, if you breathe it for too long, you'll run out of oxygen and pass out. If that happens while you're alone and wearing an oxygen mask, who will be there to take the mask off of you and save your life? No one. Sadly, this is an all too common cause of death from inhalants. Want to know the technical term for a death such as this? Accidental suicide.

3
The
Long-Term
Damage

As if the immediate damage done by inhalants weren't enough to send you running from the room, the damage done to a longtime inhalant abuser's body might just make you sick to your stomach! Let's take a look at each major organ in the body to see exactly how prolonged inhalant abuse damages our bodies.

Brain Damage

The toxins found in most solvent inhalants are so powerful that over time they actually change the way the neurons in your brain communicate with each other. The neurons in your brain are responsible for transmitting important information. For example, when you want to move your arm, the neurons in your brain communicate to other neurons in your brain that you want to move your arm, then your arm moves. Damaging the neurons in your brain can affect not only your

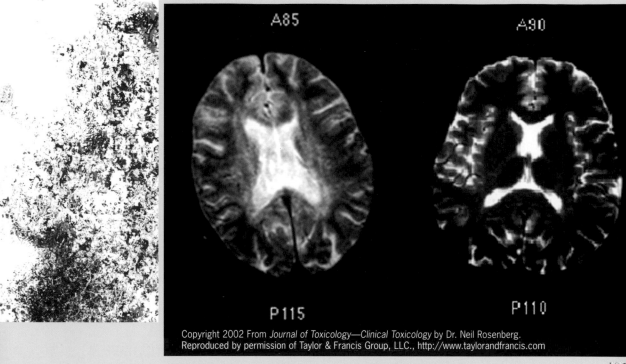

The two brain scans shown here come from young inhalant abusers. Each shows different stages of long-term, permanent brain damage caused by inhalant abuse.

motor skills but also your moods, your personality, and even your ability to learn.

Your brain and your spinal cord constitute your central nervous system, which is responsible for controlling your behavior and the way you move around and interact with the world. Inhalants have the potential of damaging your entire central nervous system, eventually slowing down brain activity in general. Drugs like heroin and alcohol work in the same fashion.

Long-term damage to your central nervous system can result in permanent numbness in varying parts of your body, overall weakness, and even muscle paralysis.

The myelin sheath is a protective coating found around cells in the central nervous system. Abuse inhalants long enough and you can permanently damage the myelin sheath, which can leave you with symptoms similar to multiple sclerosis.

Inhalants are lipophilic, which is a big fancy word that simply means "drawn to fatty tissue." This is a bad news for your brain since about 50 percent of it is made up of fat. Since fat cells are great at storing toxins inside of them, this means that inhalants have the ability to remain in your brain for a very long time.

When you get high on an inhalant, you become woozy and have a hard time walking or talking, much like a person drunk on alcohol. This is caused by the inhalant damaging the part of your brain called the cerebellum, which controls your motor skills and coordination. Damage this part of your brain too many times and the effects could be permanent. Good luck catching a baseball when your motor skills have been so damaged that it takes you a few seconds to lift your arm.

Inhalants and Your Lungs

Your lungs are very fragile organs made of thin, easily damaged tissue that are designed to breath in oxygen—and not much of anything else. Over time, inhaling toxins such as paint thinner, glue, or nail polish remover has the same effects of opening up your body and coating your lungs in a thin layer of these toxic substances. This eventually leads to something you definitely don't want, which is chemical pneumonitis.

Chemical pneumonitis is caused by severe irritation of the lungs from prolonged chemical ingestion. Chemical pneumonitis causes your lungs to swell up and fill with liquid, making you cough around the clock and even sometimes feel like you're drowning in your own body. This leads to an intense buildup of scar tissue and can eventually even lead to death.

Heart Problems

Inhalants have the ability to mess with the rhythm of your heart, confusing it into going from super fast to super slow in a matter of moments. Inhalants can also lower your ability to handle adrenaline and can cause a massive, instant heart attack. The more you mess

Inhalant abusers, even those who have used for a short period of time, can develop asthma, which they'll have for the rest of their lives.

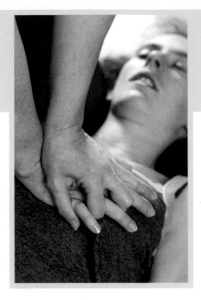

If there's no time to get medical help, CPR and other life-saving techniques can be the last hope for an inhalant addict.

with the rhythm of your heart and the more you confuse your heart with rapid changes in speed, the higher your chance of a heart attack. Long-term damage to your heart from inhalant abuse often leads to death from a painful heart attack. And you can't get any more long-term than death.

Inside Your Nose

The inside of your nose is lined with something called a mucous membrane. This is basically a protective coating inside your nose that helps fight off harmful bacteria and keeps bad things from getting inside your respiratory system. When you breathe in toxic inhalants, you are basically slowly stripping away your mucous membrane. This can lead to sores and cuts throughout the inside of your nose, chronic nosebleeds, and even gross sores around your nostrils and on your upper lip. If you think a zit looks bad on your nose, that's nothing compared to what inhalant abusers put themselves through.

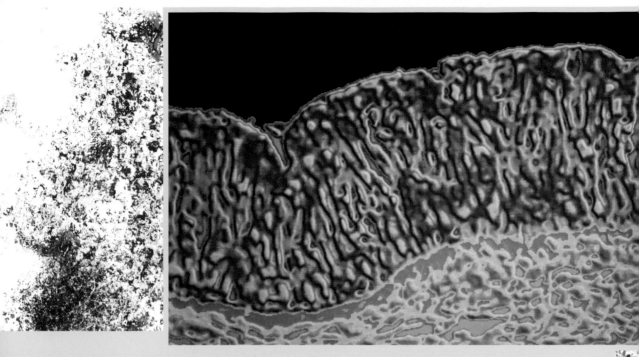

This is what the mucous membranes inside your nasal passages look like. Mess with inhalants for too long and these membranes will be eaten away, possibly destroying your sense of smell.

Other Long-Term Damage Caused by Inhalants

The following are brief explanations of other long-term damage and disease caused by prolonged inhalant abuse.

- The membranes of your kidneys can be damaged, leading to severe kidney damage and eventually death. Inhalant abuse can also cause painful kidney stones.

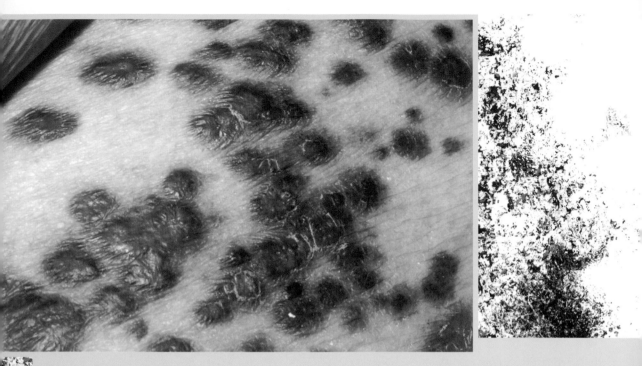

The abuse of nitrite inhalants can lead to a cancer known as Kaposi's sarcoma. One of the painful side effects is the appearance of black lesions like these on the skin.

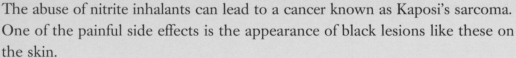

- Nitrous oxide and other anesthetics can cause serious spinal cord damage. Vitamin B12 is vital for the health of your spinal cord. Extended nitrous oxide use can prevent your body from creating enough B12, which can lead to spinal cord deterioration.
- Inhalant abuse can lead to permanent mental confusion.
- Benzene, one of the most common chemicals found in solvents, has been proven to damage bone marrow, which

can lead to a low red blood cell count (anemia) and a cancer known as leukemia.

- There is evidence that abuse of nitrite inhalants, such as poppers, can cause a type of cancer known as Kaposi's sarcoma.
- Solvent abusers can end up with a painful rash around the nose and mouth that is very hard to get rid of.
- B12 deficiency, caused by the abuse of nitrous oxide and other anesthetics, can lead to paralysis of bladder and bowel functions.

Now that we've seen the extensive and disgusting damage done to our bodies by messing around with inhalants, it's time to find out the damage inhalants can cause to our personal lives.

4
Inhalants
and Your Life

When you're a drug addict (and all inhalant abusers are), it's not just your body that you're hurting but your personal life and the personal lives of everyone around you. Like other drugs, inhalants can destroy nearly every part of your world. Inhalants can ruin your grades, damage your future, mess up your friendships, end your ability to enjoy sports, and hurt your parents and family members. As we'll find out in this chapter, just as inhalants cause destruction in nearly every part of your body, they cause just as much destruction in every part of your life as well.

A lot of people think that just because you can buy inhalants in supermarkets and drugstores, and because the high is relatively quick, that inhalants aren't addictive. This is completely untrue. Inhalants have been proven to be just as addictive as any other addictive substances, such as alcohol.

Inhalant abuse can cause rapid mood changes, lead to serious depression, leave you with a constant feeling of hopelessness, and even make you consider suicide.

The more an abuser uses inhalants, the more he or she builds up what is called a tolerance. When you have a tolerance to a drug, it means that in order to get high you have to consume larger amounts of that drug each time you use it. Maybe the first time you sniff a paint marker you'll get high right away, but the tenth time it will take sniffing that paint marker for a whole five minutes before you get that same high. Needing larger amounts of a drug every time you use it and needing to get high more often are signs of addiction and go hand in hand with inhalant abuse.

Over time, an addicted inhalant abuser will need to use inhalants many times a day in order to not go into what is called withdrawal. Withdrawal happens when your brain and body aren't getting enough of a chemical that they're used to getting. If your brain and body are used to getting high on toxic inhalants all the time, then your brain and body will show signs of withdrawal the moment they're not getting the drug they're used to getting. Signs of withdrawal include depression, hallucinations, violent behavior, headaches, and chills.

Inhalant abusers often complain of feelings of hopelessness, severe depression, and even unexpected moments of rage and violent behavior. Moods like these can even lead to thoughts of suicide.

Inhalants as Gateway Drugs

A gateway drug is a drug that often leads to the user experimenting with multiple drugs. Many inhalant users, even after trying inhalants only a few times, go on to mess around with other dangerous and potentially deadly drugs. Since inhalants are usually inexpensive and the high doesn't last very long, inhalant users often find themselves wanting longer and more powerful highs.

Inhalant abusers can very easily and very quickly end up becoming alcoholics or heroin addicts, or addicted to many different drugs at once. Messing around with inhalants isn't just risking the dangers that come along with inhalants, it's opening the door to becoming addicted to other

Suicide

Inhalant abusers often complain of feelings of hopelessness, severe depression, and even unexpected moments of rage and violent behavior. Moods like these can lead to thoughts of suicide.

dangerous and deadly drugs as well. And that's a door you definitely want to keep closed.

Inhalants and Your Social Life

Inhalant abusers often find their social lives falling apart all around them. When you're high on inhalants all the time, you care about only one thing: inhalants. You begin to care less about things that were once important to you, such as school, sports, after-school activities, your friends, even your family. Mess around with inhalants for too long and you'll soon see that your whole life begins to revolve around inhalants. You're an inhalant addict, and just as with other drug addicts, everything positive in your life is going to take a turn for the worse.

Even being addicted to inhalants for just a short time can affect your entire future. What if your grades take a big dive for a period of time and

Inhalant abuse can turn you into someone you never wanted to be. It can take control of your life and damage your most important relationships.

you end up not being able to go to the college you wanted to go to, play for the sports team you wanted to play for, or act in the school play you wanted to act in? Imagine all of the great, fun things you could be deciding not to take part in just because you wanted to get high on inhalants. Is that a decision you really want to be making when you're high in the first place?

Accidental Suicide

In chapter 2, we mentioned briefly that accidental suicide is a serious risk of inhalant abuse. Some inhalant abusers breathe in inhalants by placing a bag over their head, wearing an oxygen mask, or even holding a chemical-dipped rag in their mouth. As we already know, inhalants make you very drowsy and can sometimes even cause you to lose consciousness.

If you continue to breathe in the toxic chemicals even after you've lost consciousness, you can very easily die. Even worse, some users have lost consciousness and then died in their sleep from choking on their own vomit. Talk about horrible! Accidental suicide can happen any time to any inhalant abuser. The only way to stay safe is to stay away from inhalants.

Inhalants Cause Accidents

When you're high on inhalants, you can easily do things you'd never do when you were sober. Trying to drive a car or even ride your bike can quickly lead to not only your own death but the deaths of innocent people around you. Some inhalant users feel so good while high that they begin to think they can fly and might even be crazy enough to jump right off of a building. Talk about making a giant mistake!

Even just walking around while high on inhalants can cause you to fall and hurt yourself, trip down a flight of stairs, or injure someone walking

Inhalants can impair your judgment and cause you to do things that might seem dangerous or even crazy to you when you're sober.

near you. There's no way to say what kind of dumb decisions you'll make while high on inhalants. The only smart decision is never to try them in the first place.

Reckless Behavior

Your inhibition is a little voice in your head that lets you know what you're comfortable doing and what you're uncomfortable doing. We learn to overcome some inhibitions, like being shy, as we get older. But some inhibitions, like those we may have about our sexuality and our bodies, can be easily taken advantage of by drugs such as inhalants. Just like inhalants can cause accidental suicide and other accidents, they can also cause you to make bad decisions or to put yourself in potentially danger-ous social situations.

To put it simply, when you're high on inhalants, you increase your risk of being a victim of rape or date rape. You even leave yourself open to unwanted pregnancy and sexually transmitted disease such as HIV/AIDS. It's a scary truth, but then again, inhalants are scary drugs.

Getting Help

There is help out there for those suffering from inhalant addiction. Whether you find yourself addicted to inhalants or you know someone who has an inhalant addiction, the first step is to tell an adult that you trust. Whether it's a parent, a teacher, the principal of your school, or another adult that you feel comfortable turning to for help, you have to make an adult aware of your inhalant addiction. That person can decide what the best form of treatment would be for you. Most likely, it will involve checking into a drug treatment and rehabilitation center, drug counseling, and maybe even therapy.

Getting off of drugs is a hard, long road, but it sure beats the alternative: continuing to be a drug addict and eventually dying of an overdose or a drug-related illness.

If you suspect a friend of having an inhalant abuse problem but aren't quite sure how to tell if your friend is indeed messing around with inhalants, here are a few warning signs to look for.

- Chemical smell to his or her breath and/or clothing
- Sudden mood swings
- Stumbling when he or she walks and/or slurring of speech
- Sores/rashes under his or her nose and/or upper lip
- Unusual shortness of breath

There is nothing fun or harmless about inhalants, and there is never a good reason to follow your friends and try them. The safest decision is never to experiment with inhalants in the first place.

- Serious change in personality
- A newfound need to be alone a majority of the time
- Hanging out with a new group of people known to mess around with drugs

Your friend may not have all of these symptoms or may have slightly different symptoms, so the best way to find out if someone you know has a problem with inhalants is to ask that person as a friend. Remind the person that he or she can trust you and that you only want to help your friend be the best person possible. You may just be saving your friend's life.

Final Thoughts

You can now see the disgusting damage inhalants can cause to not just your body but every part of your life as well. Messing around with inhalants doesn't just affect you, it affects everyone around you. Think of how many people in this world would be affected if something happened to you because of inhalant abuse. Think of all the great things you could be throwing down the drain because of inhalant abuse. After thinking about it for just a few moments, you'll probably agree that the risks of inhalant abuse are just too high to even consider trying inhalants one time.

Whether you're going through a hard time in your life and think inhalants will make you happier, or you feel peer pressure because people around you are trying inhalants, or you feel angry and want to rebel against your parents or other people around you, trying inhalants is never the answer. Try talking to a parent or friend, reading a book, or playing sports. When you mess with inhalants, even just once, you open the door to all of the disgusting and terrifying things you've learned about in this book. Stay safe. Stay healthy. And remember, the warning labels are telling the truth!

Glossary

aerosol A container that sprays out a substance held under pressure. Many inhalants come in aerosol containers.

anesthetic A gas usually used by doctors to help prevent pain or make someone unconscious for surgery. Some anesthetics are used by inhalant abusers.

huffing The act of breathing in an inhalant by putting the substance into a bag or onto a rag and then breathing for periods of time directly from that bag or rag.

lipophilic Substances that are drawn to fatty cells in your body. Inhalants are lipophilic.

neurons Cells found in the central nervous system (the brain and the spinal cord) that transmit information to one another, informing your body how to behave.

nitrite A type of inhalant, nitrites are usually used to help prevent heart attacks in patients at high risk for heart attacks. When used by inhalant abusers, they might be called poppers.

solvent Any substance that helps dissolve another substance. Many inhalants are solvents, such as gasoline, glue, and paint thinner.

tolerance When a user's body builds up a resistance to a drug and therefore the user has to use more and more of that drug in order to get high.

For More Information

American Council for Drug Education (ACDE)
164 W. 74th Street
New York, NY 10023
(800) 488-DRUG (488-3784)
Web site: http://www.acde.org

Center for Substance Abuse Treatment (CSAT)
Information and Treatment Referral Hotline
11426 Rockville Pilke, Suite 410
Rockville, MD 20852
(800) 662-HELP (622-4357)
Web site: http://csat.samhsa.gov

D.A.R.E (Drug Abuse Resistance Education)
9800 LA Cienega Boulevard, Suite 401
Inglewood, CA 90301
(800) 223-DARE (223-3273)
Web site: http://www.dare.com

National Inhalant Prevention Coalition (NIPC)
332-A Thompson Street
Chattanooga, TN 37405

(800) 269-4237

Web site: http://www.inhalants.org

Substance Abuse and Mental Health Services Administration (SAMHSA)

1 Choke Cherry Road

Rockville, MD 20857

(240) 276-2000

Web site: http://www.samhsa.gov

Web Sites

Due to the changing nature of Internet links, Rosen Publishing has developed an online list of Web sites related to the subject of this book. This site is updated regularly. Please use this link to access the list:

http://www.rosenlinks.com/idd/inab

For Further Reading

Bankston, John. *Inhalants=Busted*. Berkeley Heights, NJ: Enslow Publishers, 2006.

Bayer, Linda N. *Inhalants* (Junior Drug Awareness). Philadelphia, PA: Chelsea House Publishers, 2000.

Falkowski, Carol. *Dangerous Drugs: An Easy to Use Reference for Parents and Professionals*. 2nd ed. Minneapolis, MN: Hazelden, 2000.

Gahlinger, Paul M. *Illegal Drugs: A Complete Guide to Their History, Chemistry, Use and Abuse*. New York, NY: Plume, 2003.

Kuhn, Cynthia, Scott Swartzwelder, and Wilkie Wilson. *Buzzed: The Straight Facts About the Most Used and Abused Drugs from Alcohol to Ecstasy*. New York, NY: W. W. Norton & Company, Inc., 1998.

Lobo, Ingrid A. *Inhalants* (Drugs: The Straight Facts). Philadelphia, PA: Chelsea House Publishers, 2004.

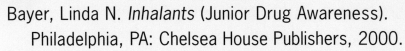

Bibliography

Bayer, Linda N. *Inhalants* (Junior Drug Awareness).
Philadelphia, PA: Chelsea House Publishers, 2000.

Julien, Robert M. *A Primer of Drug Action: A Concise,
Nontechnical Guide to the Actions, Uses, and Side Effects of
Psychoactive Drugs.* New York, NY: Worth Publishers, 2001.

Kittleson, Mark J. *The Truth About Drugs.* New York, NY: Facts
on File, 2005.

Kuhn, Cynthia, Scott Swartzwelder, and Wilkie Wilson. *Buzzed:
The Straight Facts About the Most Used and Abused Drugs
from Alcohol to Ecstasy.* New York, NY: W. W. Norton &
Company, Inc., 1998.

Lobo, Ingrid A. *Inhalants* (Drugs: The Straight Facts).
Philadelphia, PA: Chelsea House Publishers, 2004.

Menhard, Francha Roffe. *The Facts About Inhalants.* New York,
NY: Benchmark Books, 2005.

Weatherly, Myra. *Inhalants.* Springfield, NJ: Enslow
Publishers, 1996.

Weil, Andrew, and Winifred Rosen. *From Chocolate to Morphine:
Everything You Need to Know About Mind-Altering Drugs.*
New York, NY: Houghton Mifflin, 1983.

Index

About the Author

Matthew Robinson is a screenwriter and novelist living and working in Los Angeles, California. He has spent the last four years working for the Starlight/Starbright non-profit organization, mentoring sick and terminally ill children. Robinson has seen firsthand the effects of many of the diseases and illnesses caused by inhalant abuse, and therefore takes great interest in helping to educate and prevent inhalant abuse among kids nationwide.

Photo Credits

Cover, p. 1 © www.istockphoto.com/Felix Alim; p. 7 Library of Congress Prints and Photographs Division; p. 9 © Custom Medical Stock Photo; p. 12 Antonio Mari; pp. 14, 41 © AFP/Getty Images; p 19 © Getty Images; p. 23 © George Gardner/The Image Works; p. 27 © Coneyl Jay/Photo Researchers, Inc.; p. 28 © Alix/Photo Researchers, Inc.; p. 29 © Alfred Pasieka/Photo Researchers, Inc.; p. 30 National Cancer Institute; p. 33 © www.istockphoto.com/Diane Diederich; p. 36 © John Powell/Topham/The Image Works; p. 38 Shutterstock.com.

Designer: Les Kanturek; **Editor:** Nicholas Croce;
Photo Researcher: Cindy Reiman